EMMA LIGHTS THE SKY

Written and illustrated by LOU ALPERT

Whispering Coyote Press Inc./New York

Published by Whispering Coyote Press Inc.
P.O. Box 2159, Halesite, New York 11743-2159
Text copyright © 1991 by Lou Alpert
Illustrations copyright © 1991 by Lou Alpert
Printed in the United States of America
ISBN 1-879085-03-8

For Spencer, with all my love, dreams, and wishes.

At eight o'clock
      I get ready for bed.
After my kisses
      and prayers are said,

I close my eyes
and pretend to sleep.
Mom looks in,
but I don't make a peep.

My eyes open wide
   and my room becomes–

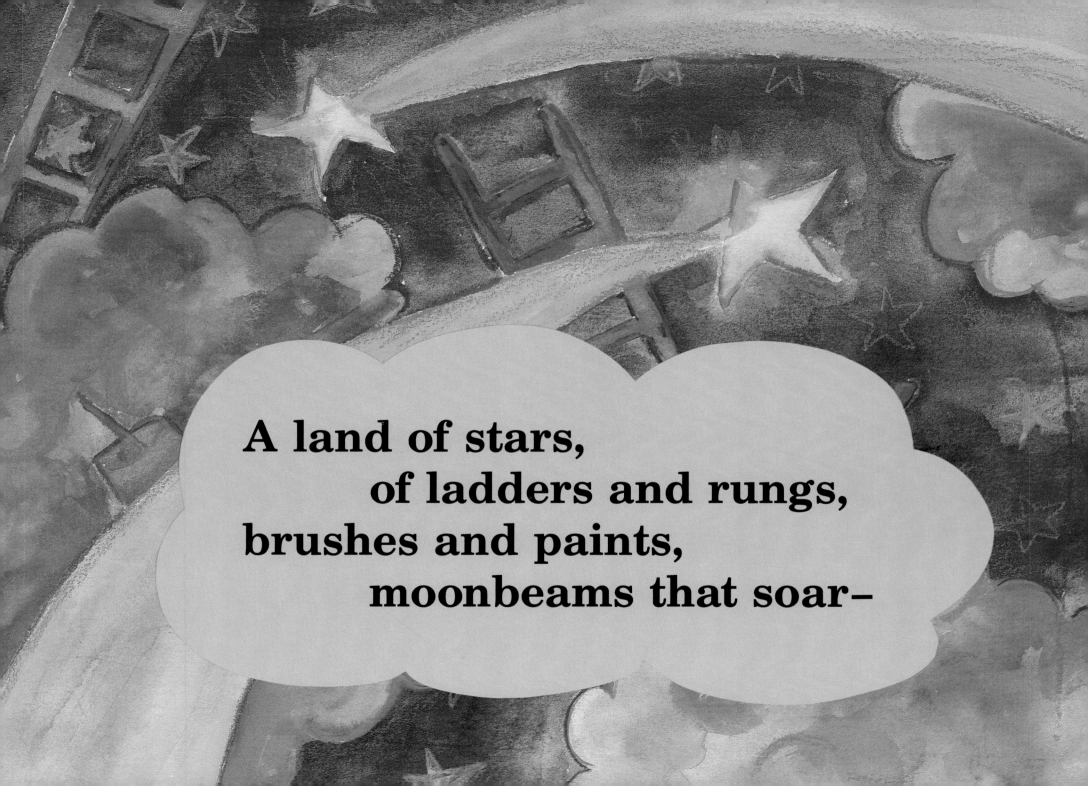

A land of stars,
　　of ladders and rungs,
brushes and paints,
　　moonbeams that soar–

It's here that I meet
        with my friends every night,
to take fallen stars
        and give them new light.

When the fire burns out
of a star in the night,
it falls to the ground
and lands out of sight.

But animals see
the stars fall from above,

And bring them to children
to light up with love.

While parents sleep snugly
throughout the land,
we gather the stars
in our loving hands.

Kiss them to light them,
and then say good-bye.

The man in the moon
takes his magical bow,

I sneak back to bed
and closing my eyes,

I sleep till the sun
rises up in the sky.